Dedicated to the real Miss Todd,
and all those who dare to dream.

MISS TODD
AND HER WONDERFUL FLYING MACHINE

Written by:
Frances Poletti & Kristina Yee

Illustrations by:
Kristina Yee, Isona Rigau & Nick Cooke

The first time Miss Lily Todd knew she wanted to fly was when she felt the wind in her hair as Grandpa Joe tossed her high into the air. From that moment on, Lily was happiest when her feet weren't touching the ground.

Lily was determined—sometimes even reckless—in her pursuit of flight. Watching birds soaring in the sky, she made her own wings. She did things that made Grandpa Joe very worried indeed!

"You're a smart girl, Lily," he would say, "but even baby birds have to *learn* how to fly."

Lily trusted her Grandpa, and started reading as much as she could about birds, bats, bees, and anything else with wings.

As Lily grew, so did her passion for flying. She discovered that wearing wings wasn't enough—if she wanted to fly, she'd have

She made lots of paper planes to test her designs, but again and again they crashed to the ground.

Whenever Lily was feeling discouraged, Grandpa Joe would pick up the pieces and tell her to try again.

But she wanted more. She was ready to stretch her wings.

"Lily?" called Grandpa Joe from the top of the stairs.

"Wish me luck, Grandpa!" said Lily as she rushed out of the house, her arms full of designs for her flying machine. It was

And she knew exactly where to go: a university! There, she could learn with others who shared her passion for flying.

But everywhere she went doors closed in her face.
All she heard was "NO, NO, NO!!!"

"Why not?" questioned Lily.

"No GIRLS allowed! That's the rule!" they all said. The universities wouldn't even give her a chance.

But then, a different voice said, "NO, NO, NO!!!"

It was Mrs. Sage, one of the richest and most important women in New York. She was sick and tired of girls not being allowed to learn and she wouldn't give another dime to any place with such silly rules.

CLEPHEN
BUILDING
EST. 1833

"And who are you?" she asked, pointing to Lily.

"I'm Miss Lily Todd."

"Come now—I don't know how you can stand to be here another second!" And with that, Mrs. Sage whisked her away.

That afternoon, Lily shared all of her hopes and dreams with Mrs. Sage. She talked through the designs for her machine, how she longed to build it, and to fly in the world-famous Long Island Flying Competition. Very soon, pilots from all over would be gathering to compete, and Lily wanted to be one of them!

Mrs. Sage believed in Lily, and knew just how she could help.

Mrs. Sage provided Lily with everything she needed to make her flying machine, including a workshop. Lily rolled up her sleeves and got to work—not that it was easy. Her hands became as rough as sandpaper, her back ached from carrying the wood, and some days it seemed like nothing was going according to plan. But she never gave up.

And then, at last...

SHE DID IT!

And just in time for the day of the competition, where pilots were getting ready to risk their necks to test their flying machines.

The machines came in all shapes and sizes,
and most of them didn't work at all.

Lily was ready to take to the skies. But "NO, NO, NO!!!" a new voice said.

"Who are you?" asked Lily.

"I'm Didier Masson, the most famous pilot in the world, and I'll be the one flying your plane today!"

"What?! Why?" exclaimed Lily.

"No girls allowed in the sky! That's the rule, and there's nothing you can do about it!"

It just wasn't fair, Lily thought.

But then, Lily had an idea.

Snatching Didier's scarf and helmet, she decided to take things into her own hands…

Too late for anyone to stop her now! But would Lily fly?

SHE WAS FLYING!

She had done it! She'd
proved them all wrong!

SNAP!

But oh dear! Lily was in trouble. A snap in the wing. Would she end up like all of the other pilots whose flying machines had crashed to the ground?

She couldn't give up now! Lily gripped the steering wheel and gritted her teeth. The frame shuddered and creaked, but she held on until she could feel herself gliding on the wind as gracefully as the birds she used to watch from her window. She felt freer than she had ever felt before.

The ground rushed towards her as she came in for a landing. Lily braced herself...

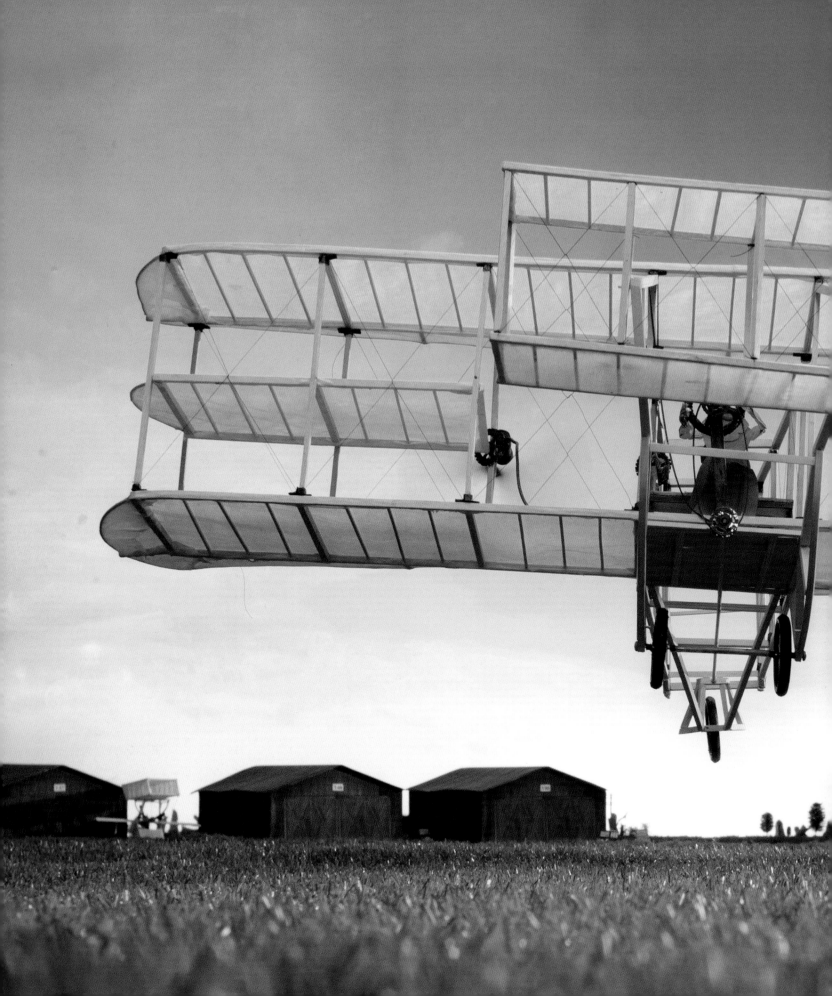

She landed! Her machine had flown and she had felt the wind in her hair before safely returning to the ground. Lily felt invincible.

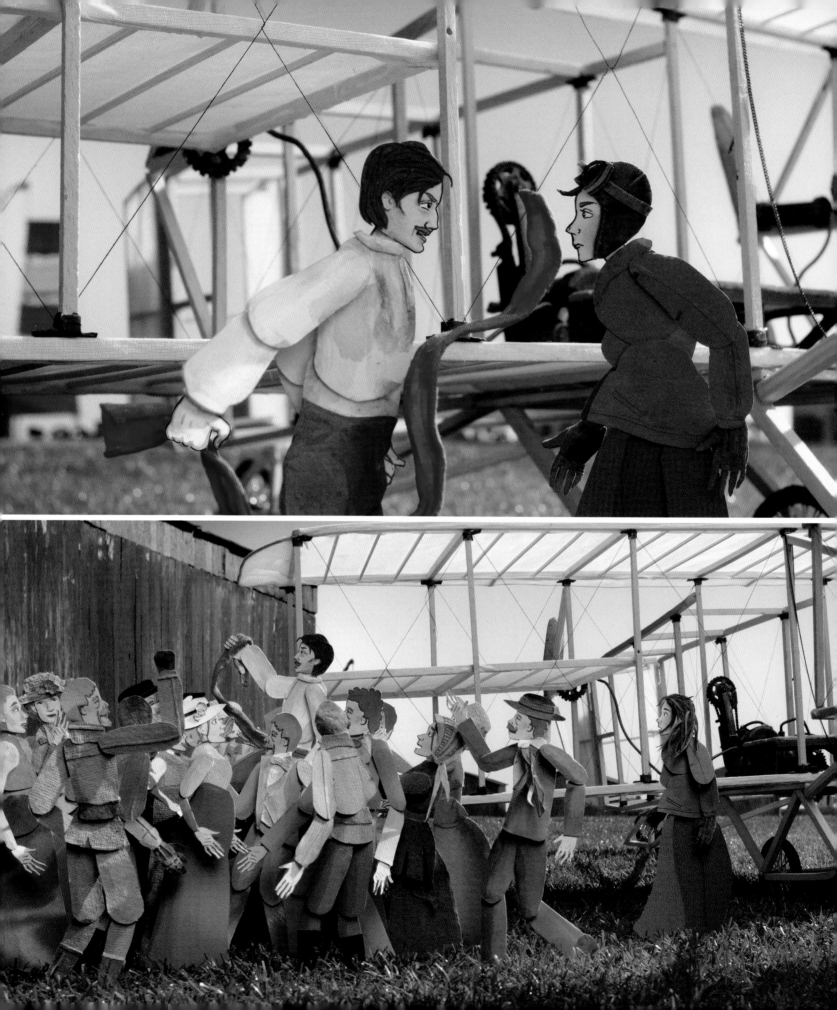

A furious Didier was waiting, snatching back his scarf and cap. "You!" he growled.

"I did it," Lily exclaimed, "I flew!"

"No you didn't! It's against the rules and doesn't count! Women don't fly," taunted Didier.

The cheering crowd rushed in— but oh, no, no no! They lifted *Didier* onto their shoulders, believing *he* had been piloting the plane all along, in his famous red scarf.

As they carried him away, chanting his name, Lily was left alone on the airfield.

Her heart was broken. She felt that in all the world, the only words that were left for her were "no, no, no."

What was she to do if her dreams were against the rules?

As Lily sat amongst her beloved books, the paper worn thin from studying and model planes surrounding her, she knew she couldn't give up. After everything she had fought for, all that she had achieved, and with the sky still beckoning, she had to fly again.

So that's just what Lily did. She realized that it didn't matter what other people said—she would always find a way. And when she was soaring high above the clouds, flying free with the wind in her hair, she knew that nothing could hold her down—not even gravity.

THE REAL PEOPLE

Miss Todd and Her Wonderful Flying Machine is a work of fiction inspired by the real 1910 flight of a plane designed by Miss E. Lilian Todd. Though this book is a flight of fancy, Miss Todd, Mrs. Sage, and Didier Masson were real people who contributed to humankind's discovery and mastery of flight.

MISS TODD:
Miss E. Lilian Todd (1865–1937) was acknowledged by the *New York Times* on November 28, 1909 as the first woman in the world to build and design an airplane. She was an inventor, a student of law, and a dreamer. After the successful flight of her first plane, she never built another and, as far we know, never flew.

MRS. SAGE:
Mrs. Margaret Olivia Slocum Sage (1828–1918) was married to financier and railroad executive Russell Sage. Upon his death, she inherited a fortune of more than $50,000,000, which she invested in philanthropic endeavors. In particular, she supported education and the advancement of women such as Miss Lily Todd, founding schools and scholarships in her husband's name.

MR. DIDIER MASSON:
Didier Masson (1886–1950) was a French aviator, pioneering barnstormer, and combat pilot. In the First World War, he shot down an enemy aircraft after his own plane's motor quit running, glided to land in enemy territory, and found his way back onto friendly soil. Didier was also the first aviator to deliver newspapers by air, setting the world's longest non-stop distance record in the process.

THE FILM BEHIND THE STORY

Before *Miss Todd and Her Wonderful Flying Machine* was a book, it was a short, animated musical film made by a group of passionate students, led by director Kristina Yee at the National Film and Television School in the United Kingdom.

It took a full year for them to make the twelve-minute short, which went on to win a Student Academy Award in 2013, a Royal Television Society Award in 2014, and play at dozens of festivals around the world.

The director, Kristina Yee, wants to thank all of the people who made *Miss Todd* possible with their hearts, minds, and hands.

THE WONDERFUL TEAM:
Producer Suzanne Mayger
Writers Frances Poletti and Kristina Yee
Cinematographer Nick Cooke
Production Designer Isona Rigau
Editor Michele Chiappa
Composer Matt Kelly
Sound Designer Tom Lock Griffiths
Colorist and VFX Supervisor Kamaljit Bains
VFX Supervisor Phil Chapman
Artistic Coordinator Pallavi Davé
Supervising Art Director Laura Mickiewicz
Production Manager Georgia Orwell

CAST:
Lucie Jones as Miss Todd
Joy McBrinn as Mrs. Sage
Peter Marinker as Grandpa Joe
Tristan Chenais as Mr. Didier Masson

For a full list of credits and to find out more about the film, visit www.misstoddfilm.com.

COMPENDIUM.
live inspired

CREDITS:

Written by: Frances Poletti & Kristina Yee

Illustrated by: Kristina Yee, Isona Rigau & Nick Cooke

Designed by: Helen Tsao

Edited by: Amelia Riedler

Creative Direction by: Julie Flahiff

With special thanks to the National Film and Television School and the entire Compendium family.

NFTS | **NATIONAL FILM AND TELEVISION SCHOOL**

Library of Congress Control Number: 2014959334

ISBN: 978-1-938298-76-9

1st printing. Printed in China with soy inks. A021503001